Debbie.

THE BLUEBERRY TRAIN

by C. L. G. Martin

illustrated by

Angela Trotta Thomas

ATHENEUM BOOKS FOR YOUNG READERS

ATHENEUM BOOKS FOR YOUNG READERS
An imprint of Simon & Schuster Children's Publishing Division
1230 Avenue of the Americas, New York, New York 10020
Text copyright © 1995 by C. L. G. Martin
Illustrations copyright © 1995 by Angela Trotta Thomas
Book design by Carolyn Boschi
The text for this book is set in Simonici Garamond.
The illustrations are rendered in watercolor.
Manufactured in Hong Kong
First edition
10 9 8 7 6 5 4 3 2 1

LIBRARY OF CONGRESS CATALOGING-IN-PUBLICATION DATA

Martin, C. L. G.
The blueberry train / C. L. G. Martin ;
illustrated by Angela Trotta Thomas. — 1st ed.   p.   cm.
Summary: In Minnesota in the 1920s, a young boy wants to
go to pick blueberries all by himself to prove to his mother
that he is not a baby any longer.
ISBN 0-689-80304-4
[1. Mothers and sons—Fiction.   2. Blueberries—Fiction.]
I. Thomas, Angela Trotta, ill.   II. Title.
PZ7.M356776Bl   1995   [E]—dc20   93-31014

To my best friends, Cindy and Jaci

C. M.

To my father, Anthony Trotta, and
special thanks to Bernie, Tom, and Bobby

A. T. T.

*L*ouis turned to wave one last wave as Pa's ore boat sailed into the sun.

"Keep both hands on the handle-bars, Louis."

Louis felt angry. "You're not my boss," he grumbled to his older brother.

"Now, Louis," said Ma softly. "Willie is the man of the house for the summer."

"And I'll take care of everything," Willie proclaimed.

"*I* don't need taking care of," Louis snapped. He pointed his bicycle downhill, pedaled furiously, and threw his arms out to the wind.

He was an eagle flying,
soaring,
diving—

and crashing into the ground.

"Louis! What's gotten into you?" Ma scolded him, gently swabbing his bloody knees. "Your pants are ruined!"

Louis was suddenly hopeful. "Can I get long pants like Willie, Ma? Please?"

"Little boys wear short pants, Louis."

Louis pouted. "I am *not* a little boy," he said.

At the bottom of the hill, a train pulled into the depot. Louis stretched out to feel the ground rumble against his stomach.

"The blueberries must be ripe already," said Ma. "It's the blueberry train."

Louis's hopes rose again. "Ma, can I go on the blueberry train? I could pick enough blueberries to buy new pants. Please, Ma? I can take care of myself. I'm not a baby."

"Copper Creek is so far away," Ma said.

"Please, Ma."

"You've never ridden on a train before."

"*Please,* Ma. Let me go tomorrow."

Ma sighed. "All right, Louis."

Louis blinked in disbelief.

Below them, the blueberry train rumbled out of the station like a hissing, screeching, fire-breathing dragon. It slithered over the bridge across the bay. Suddenly Louis didn't feel so brave.

The day went by much too quickly, and the night was filled with dreams of dragons, black knights, and dark, gloomy dungeons. Louis tossed and turned till morning.

"Hurry up, Louis! You're going to miss the train," Ma called.

Louis pulled his torn, dirty knickers over clean stockings and hooked his shoes with fumbling fingers.

Ma handed Louis his lunch tin. She pulled him into her gardenia-scented hug, then pushed him toward the door. "Hurry now."

"Don't get lost," Willie mumbled through cheeks stuffed with oatmeal.

"I can take care of myself," Louis snapped, dragging his blueberry buckets out the door.

He hurried down the hill, stopping once to wave to Ma and Willie, but they were nowhere in sight.

"One, please," Louis said to the lady in the ticket cage.

"Are you all alone?" she asked with obvious concern.

"I can take c-care of myself," said Louis. He paid for his ticket and followed the other blueberry people down to the train.

"All aboard!" yelled the conductor.

Louis jumped at the sound of a squeaky voice.

"Do you mind if I sit?" asked a lady in an enormous hat that trailed a billowy white veil. "Trains scare me—all the smoke and noise. I would feel so much better with a strong young man like yourself as my seat companion."

The blueberry lady sat, arranging the smoky white veil over her face. "Sunshine is good for blueberries, but not the complexion," she explained.

Louis stared at her curiously. There was no sunshine in the train.

The train lurched forward, and a young man stumbled into the facing seat. He wore a baseball cap pulled down to his ears and a woolen muffler wrapped up to his eyes. He had four blueberry buckets. "Hello," he mumbled in a gravelly voice.

"Aren't you hot?" Louis asked.

"Flowers make me sneeze," mumbled the tall young man. "I have to keep the pollen out of my nose."

Louis stared at him curiously. There were no flowers on the train.

The train gathered speed and rolled over the wooden bridge with a thunderous *clackety-clack*. The water looked very far below.

"Goodness!" said the lady. "I had no idea this bridge was so high! Would you hold my hand? It would make me feel so much better."

Louis slipped his fingers into her warm, friendly hand.

The train clattered through the woods and charged past farms and ponds and grazing cattle, whistling a frantic warning: Look out! I'm coming!

When it shuddered and shook and finally slowed, Louis pulled back his hand and sat straight in his seat.

"Copper Creek!" yelled the conductor.

Louis joined the people bumping down the aisle with their baskets and buckets.

"Back at five!" the conductor called.

Louis felt all alone in the woods full of blueberry people.

"Perhaps we could pick together," suggested the blueberry lady.

Louis knelt shyly beside her and began plucking the waxy blueberries from their sturdy little bushes.

The sun climbed in the sky, and sweat dripped off the end of his nose. His fingers felt numb, but he didn't mind. Tomorrow he would sell his blueberries to Hemplemier's Bakery. Then he'd march next door to Cromwell's Department Store and plunk his money on the counter for a pair of long pants. He could take care of himself!

"Let's eat," said the lady cheerfully. She unwrapped an oatmeal-bread sandwich stuffed with ham, as did the young man, who ate it under his woolly scarf.

Louis bit into his sandwich and stared at them suspiciously.

The blueberry lady fanned her face with a lace hanky. Louis caught the slightest whiff of gardenias.

The blueberry young man gobbled his food, swelling his woolly muffler out over sandwich-stuffed cheeks.

"I'm going to get back to work," Louis announced suddenly, jumping to his feet.

"I have to pick enough blueberries to pay for a pair of long pants so my family will stop treating me like a baby. My brother didn't get long pants until he was twelve! What do you think of *that*?" Louis asked of the woolly muffler.

The woolly muffler coughed.

Louis lugged his buckets to a far corner of the clearing and down a trampled path. I'll find my own stand of bushes, he thought. I'll pick enough blueberries to buy long pants *and* a tie *and* a pocket watch. I'll show them!

Overhanging pine trees cast dark shadows across the path. Louis could not hear the chatter of the other blueberry pickers, but something was watching him. He could feel it in his bones.

Behind him, the bushes shook. Louis whirled around. Out toddled a baby black bear not much bigger than a puppy.

Louis caught his breath. "Hi, boy," he croaked. "Are you lost?"

Before he could take another step, the bushes exploded with a snarling, snorting mother bear. The mother grunted angrily, and the baby bear climbed a tree.

Louis's heart fell into his stomach. He couldn't breathe! He couldn't move! He closed his eyes.

"Shoo!" yelled a voice. "Shoo!"

"Nice bear. Nice bear," called a second voice.

Louis opened his eyes. His blueberry mother and his blueberry brother ran toward him, clanging their buckets.

The mother bear reared up on her hind legs and bellowed.

"Ma!" Louis shrieked. "Willie!"

"Run!" screamed Ma.

"Run!" screamed Willie.

And they ran. They ran helter-skelter through the scratchy forest all the way back to the train tracks.

Louis gasped for air. "Why was . . . that bear . . . so mad?" he asked, panting.

"Because . . . nothing's more precious . . . to a mama . . . than her baby," Ma replied. She took a deep breath.

"Mothers protect their young. It's a law of nature."

Louis let Ma hug him, even in front of all the people.

"You knew it was us all along, didn't you?" Willie said, scratching at a rash he'd gotten from wearing the muffler.

Louis shook his head.

"Are you angry that we followed you?" Ma asked apologetically. Her hat sat lopsided on her head, its enormous brim and veil resting in tatters around her neck.

Louis grinned. How could he be mad at two such rumpled, crumpled-looking people?

The blueberry train whistled, and the blueberry people started to take their brimming buckets and baskets home.

The buckets! Louis spun around. They had left their buckets near the bear!

"Never mind, Louis," Ma said. "Today you rode the blueberry train all by yourself. You even escaped from a bear! And you did it all in short pants."

"That's right," said Louis, grinning proudly. "So you won't treat me like a baby anymore?"

"I'll try." Ma smiled. "But, Louis, don't you know? You'll always be my baby."

Louis sighed. He leaned into Ma's gardenia-scented hug and let the blueberry train rock him gently to sleep.